ROBIN HOOD

OUTLAW OF SHERWOOD FOREST

AN
ENGLISH
LEGEND

STORY BY
PAUL D. STORRIE

PENCILS AND INKS BY
THOMAS YEATES

ROBIN HOOD

OUTLAW OF SHERWOOD FOREST

AN
ENGLISH
LEGEND

IRISH
SEA

NOTTINGHAMSHIRE
(HOME OF SHERWOOD FOREST)

. NOTTINGHAM

ENGLAND

GRAPHIC UNIVERSE™ • MINNEAPOLIS

ROBIN HOOD MAY OR MAY NOT HAVE BEEN AN ACTUAL PERSON. REAL OR NOT, HIS ADVENTURES HAVE DELIGHTED READERS, LISTENERS, AND VIEWERS FOR CENTURIES. TO WRITE THIS PARTICULAR BOOK, AUTHOR PAUL D. STORRIE RELIED HEAVILY ON THE EARLIEST VERSIONS OF THE ROBIN HOOD STORIES AVAILABLE: THE LYRICS TO THE MEDIEVAL SONGS ABOUT ROBIN AND HIS FOLLOWERS. HIS RESEARCH ALSO INCLUDED THE EXCELLENT BOOKS *ROBIN HOOD* BY J. C. HOLT AND *ROBIN HOOD: A COMPLETE STUDY OF THE ENGLISH OUTLAW* BY STEPHEN THOMAS KNIGHT. ARTIST THOMAS YEATES REFERRED TO BOOKS BY GREAT ILLUSTRATORS OF THE PAST, INCLUDING HOWARD PYLE, HAROLD FOSTER, AND N. C. WYETH.

STORY BY PAUL D. STORRIE

PENCILS AND INKS BY THOMAS YEATES
WITH TOD SMITH AND KEN HOOPER

COLORING BY HI-FI DESIGN

LETTERING BY BILL HAUSER

CONSULTANT: ANDREW SCHEIL
ASSISTANT PROFESSOR OF ENGLISH,
UNIVERSITY OF MINNESOTA

Graphic Universe™
An imprint of Lerner Publishing Group, Inc.
241 First Avenue North
Minneapolis, MN 55401 U.S.A.

Website address: www.lernerbooks.com

Library of Congress Cataloging-in-Publication Data

Storrie, Paul D.
    Robin Hood : outlaw of Sherwood Forest / by Paul D. Storrie ; illustrations by Thomas Yeates.
        p.   cm. — (Graphic myths and legends)
    Summary: Recounts the life and adventures of Robin Hood, who, with his band of followers, lived in Sherwood Forest as an outlaw dedicated to fighting tyranny. Presented in comic book format.
        ISBN-13: 978-0-8225-5964-1 (lib. bdg. : alk. paper)
        ISBN-10: 0-8225-5964-1 (lib. bdg. : alk. paper)
        1. Robin Hood (Legendary character)—Legends.
    [1. Robin Hood (Legendary character)—Legends.
    2. Folklore—England. 3. Cartoons and comics.]
    I. Yeates, Thomas, ill. II. Robin Hood (Legend)
    III. Title. IV. Series.
    PZ8.1.S8845Ro 2007
    [398.2]—dc22   2006003707

Manufactured in the United States of America
1 2 3 4 5 6 7 — JR — 12 12 11 10 09 08

TABLE OF CONTENTS

HOW ROBIN CAME TO SHERWOOD

NOW LISTEN CLOSELY, GENTLE FRIENDS, ALL THOSE WHOSE HEARTS ARE GOOD; AND YOU SHALL HEAR OF A BRAVE YEOMAN, HIS NAME WAS ROBIN HOOD.

LONG AGO, IN THE KINGDOM OF ENGLAND, THERE LIVED A MAN NAMED ROBIN HOOD, THE GREATEST ARCHER THAT EVER LIVED. ALTHOUGH HE WAS AN OUTLAW, HE ONLY ROBBED THOSE WHO WERE CRUEL TO POOR AND HONEST FOLK.

BUT BEFORE HE WAS AN OUTLAW, HE WAS JUST A YOUNG MAN WITH HIGH HOPES FOR THE FUTURE. THOSE HOPES LED HIM, ONE BRIGHT MAY MORNING, TO LEAVE HIS HOME IN THE VILLAGE OF LOCKSLEY AND CUT THROUGH SHERWOOD FOREST ON HIS WAY TO THE TOWN OF NOTTINGHAM.

A CHEAT, A COWARD, AND A BAD ARCHER!

STILL, EVEN A BAD ARCHER CAN MAKE A LUCKY SHOT!

EVEN THOUGH HIS SHOTS FELL SHORT, THE FORESTERS KNEW THAT ROBIN COULD HIT ANY OF THEM AS EASILY AS HE HAD THE DEER. THEY SCRAMBLED TO HIDE BEFORE HE CHANGED HIS MIND AND TOOK BETTER AIM.

THAT SHOULD GIVE THEM PAUSE. TIME I WAS AWAY.

NOW YOU'VE DONE IT, ROBIN HOOD. AS IF KILLING ONE OF THE KING'S DEER WASN'T ENOUGH, YOU'VE FIRED ON THE KING'S FORESTERS.

YOU'RE OUTLAWED FOR CERTAIN.

NO GOING HOME NOW. IT'S LIFE IN SHERWOOD FOR YOU.

AT LEAST YOU'LL HAVE GOOD COMPANY, THEN!

13

MAYBE IT'S TIME I WENT OUT AND LOOKED FOR SOME *ADVENTURE!*

WE'LL COME WITH YOU, ROBIN.

NO NEED. I'LL BE FINE ON MY OWN.

I PROMISE THAT IF I'M IN TROUBLE, I'LL BLOW THREE NOTES ON MY HUNTING HORN. IF YOU HEAR THAT, COME RUNNING!

ROBIN WALKED THROUGH THE FOREST FOR HOURS, CHECKING THE ROADS AND PATHS FOR TRAVELERS, BUT HE WAS BEGINNING TO THINK HE WAS THE ONLY ONE OUT AND ABOUT ON THAT FINE AUTUMN DAY.

OH HO! IT LOOKS LIKE ONE OF THE TREES HAS DECIDED TO TAKE A STROLL. I'D BEST MOVE QUICKLY IF I WANT TO REACH THE BRIDGE BEFORE HIM!

BUT WHEN THE TALL STRANGER SAW THAT ROBIN MEANT TO CROSS FIRST, HE HURRIED TO THE BRIDGE TOO.

STAND BACK, MY TOWERING FRIEND, SO I MAY CROSS!

HA! IT WOULD TAKE A BETTER MAN THAN *YOU* TO MAKE *ME* STEP ASIDE! YOU CAN CROSS AFTER ME.

24

WHILE ROBIN SOLD HIS WARES, THE SHERIFF OF NOTTINGHAM'S WIFE CAME BY WITH MARIAN FITZWALTER, THE DAUGHTER OF A LOCAL LORD.

IT IS A SHAME, MARIAN, THAT THIS JOLLY POTTER CHARGES EXTRA FOR THE NOBILITY.

I LIKE HIS SPIRIT, BUT NOT HIS PRICE!

TARRY A MOMENT, GOOD LADY, PLEASE!

YOU ARE NOTHING LIKE THE STRUTTING NOBLES THAT I DISLIKE, AND AN HONEST WIFE CAN BE FOUND IN PEASANT'S SHACK OR KNIGHT'S MANOR!

WHAT ABOUT THE SHERIFF'S HALL?

ARE YOU OUR GOOD SHERIFF'S WIFE? FOR THAT ALONE, I WOULD GIVE YOU A SPECIAL PRICE!

IF YOU WILL TELL ME THE NAME OF THE BEAUTIFUL GIRL WITH YOU, I'LL GIVE YOU HALF OF WHAT I HAVE LEFT FOR FREE.

AND IF YOU CAN GET HER TO GIVE ME A KISS, SHE CAN HAVE THE REST!

WHY THAT'S MARIAN, THE DAUGHTER OF LORD FITZWALTER, MY HUSBAND'S FRIEND.

AS FOR THE KISS, THAT WOULD BE UP TO HER.

27

HOW COULD I REFUSE SUCH AN OFFER?

HMM. NOW HOW WILL WE GET ALL THESE POTS TO MY HOME?

I KNOW! POTTER, IF YOU WILL TAKE THEM BY CART, YOU MAY SHARE OUR SUPPER.

BESIDES, MY HUSBAND HAS BEEN IN A BAD MOOD, WHAT WITH THIS OUTLAW ROBIN HOOD CAUSING SO MUCH TROUBLE. IT WOULD DO HIM GOOD TO MEET SUCH A HAPPY SOUL!

HOW COULD I REFUSE SUCH AN OFFER?

SOON ROBIN FOUND HIMSELF AT THE SHERIFF'S TABLE. BUT SINCE THEY HAD NEVER MET, THE SHERIFF DID NOT GUESS THAT THE HUMBLE POTTER WAS THE INFAMOUS OUTLAW HE LONGED TO CAPTURE.

MY WIFE TELLS ME YOU ARE A CAREFREE SOUL, PRACTICALLY GIVING AWAY YOUR WARES!

WELL, IT JUST SEEMS TO ME THAT WHEN A MAN HAS WHAT HE NEEDS, HE SHOULD BE SATISFIED WITH THAT.

HA! SPOKEN LIKE A MAN WITH SMALL NEEDS!

YOUR WIFE SAYS *YOU* NEED CHEERING UP. SOMETHING ABOUT THIS OUTLAW, ROBIN HOOD?

I BEGIN TO HATE THAT NAME! IT'S ALL I HEAR FROM PEOPLE WHO DON'T HAVE SENSE ENOUGH TO TRAVEL WITH GUARDS WHEN THEY GO THROUGH SHERWOOD!

IF I EVER MEET THIS SCOUNDREL FACE-TO-FACE, I'LL NEVER HAVE TO HEAR HIS NAME AGAIN!

MAYBE I CAN HELP YOU THERE. YOU SEE, I KNOW THIS ROBIN HOOD.

FOR FORTY MARKS, I WILL TAKE YOU TO THE FOREST TOMORROW AND *PROMISE* YOU WILL SEE HIM.

I WOULD GLADLY PAY *TWICE* THAT. BUT TELL ME, HOW IS IT THAT YOU KNOW THIS OUTLAW?

WHY, I GREW UP WITH HIM. HE'S NEVER DONE ME ANY HARM, BUT SEEING HOW MUCH YOU WANT TO MEET HIM, WHAT ELSE CAN I DO?

JUST DON'T TAKE *TOO* MANY SOLDIERS WITH YOU. THE OUTLAWS MIGHT HEAR THEM COMING AND STAY HIDDEN.

HMMM. THAT SEEMS WISE. I WILL TAKE ONLY MY BEST MEN.

OUT OF MY WAY, YOU USELESS FOOL!

LET'S GO OUT TO THE COURTYARD AND HAVE A SHOOTING MATCH! THE BEST ARCHERS WILL GO WITH US IN THE MORNING.

INCREDIBLE! AN ARCHER AS GOOD AS YOU SHOULD BE IN MY SERVICE.

I'M FLATTERED, BUT LET'S WAIT UNTIL TOMORROW BEFORE WE SPEAK OF SUCH THINGS.

THE NEXT MORNING, ROBIN, THE SHERIFF, AND HIS MEN SET OUT FOR SHERWOOD FOREST.

QUIET, NOW. THE OUTLAWS ARE NEARBY. DON'T WORRY, THOUGH. I HAVE A WAY TO DRAW THEM OUT.

TIRRAH! TIRRAH! TIRRAH!

ARE YOU INSANE? NOW WE'LL NEVER FIND THEM!

ACTUALLY, SHERIFF...

ROBIN HOOD AND
MAID MARIAN

AFTER HIS EMBARRASSMENT, THE SHERIFF OF NOTTINGHAM TRIED EVEN HARDER TO CATCH ROBIN OR ANY OF HIS MEN. THE OUTLAWS HAD TO BE MORE CAREFUL THAN EVER. THEY POSTED MORE LOOKOUTS IN THE FOREST AND EVEN CARRIED SWORDS TO HELP PROTECT THEMSELVES.

SO WHEN A PAGE CAME SNEAKING INTO SHERWOOD NOT LONG AFTER, IT WAS NO SURPRISE THAT AN OUTLAW WAS THERE TO BLOCK THE PATH, FEARING SOME SORT OF TRAP.

YOU *MUST* TAKE ME TO ROBIN HOOD! I *HAVE* TO SPEAK WITH HIM.

HOW DO I KNOW YOU'RE NOT THE SHERIFF'S SPY? ANYTHING YOU HAVE TO SAY TO HIM, YOU CAN SAY TO ME.

I HAVE NO TIME FOR THIS!

DON'T BE FOOLISH, BOY. I DON'T WANT TO HURT YOU.

DON'T WORRY. YOU WON'T.

FOR AN HOUR, NEITHER WAS ABLE TO BEAT THE OTHER. UNTIL ...

TIRRAH! TIRRAH! TIRRAH!

FRIGHTENED OF BEING OVERWHELMED BY MORE OUTLAWS, THE PAGE STRUCK WHILE HIS FOE WAS DISTRACTED.

ARGH!!

TO MAKE HIS TRAP HARDER TO RESIST, THE SHERIFF HAD SENT MESSENGERS ALL ACROSS ENGLAND TO BRING THE BEST ARCHERS IN THE ENTIRE KINGDOM TO THE CONTEST.

HE KNEW THAT ROBIN WOULD WANT TO *PROVE* HE WAS THE BEST ARCHER IN ALL OF ENGLAND.

I TAKE IT YOU DON'T SEE HIM?

THEY'RE TOO FAR AWAY. I'LL GET A CLOSER LOOK WHEN THEY SHOOT.

DO YOU *REALLY* THINK HE'LL COME?

I'M SURE OF IT. I ONLY PRAY HE'S AS CLEVER AS HE THINKS.

THERE WERE ALMOST FIVE SCORE ARCHERS TO START. EACH SHOT ONE ARROW. TEN WHO SHOT THE BEST STAYED IN THE CONTEST.

SO, IT COMES DOWN TO YOUR MAN GILBERT, THE KING'S MAN TEPUS, AND A BEGGAR!

YES. IT SEEMS OUR BRAVE OUTLAW IS A COWARD AFTER ALL!

THAT'S NOT FAIR!

YOU CALL HIM A COWARD FOR *NOT* COMING, BUT IF HE HAD, YOU'D CALL HIM A *FOOL* IF HE'D FALLEN INTO YOUR TRAP!

MARIAN! YOU'RE BEING RUDE TO OUR HOST AND FRIEND, THE SHERIFF.

STILL, SHE HAS A POINT.

ENOUGH, ENOUGH! THE FINAL SHOOTING IS ABOUT TO START.

BEST OF LUCK TO YOU, MY FRIENDS! YOU'VE DONE SOME FINE SHOOTING TODAY.

AS HAVE YOU. GOOD LUCK.

LET'S FINISH IT.

HA! HA!

THERE'S NO WAY THE BEGGAR CAN BEAT THAT SHOT! IF MY MAN HAS TO LOSE, I'M GLAD IT WAS TO THE KING'S BEST ARCHER!

SHKKK

AMAZING! THE SHOT OF A LIFETIME! WELL DONE!

Feh! AN ACCIDENT. NO MORE.

GLOSSARY AND PRONUNCIATION GUIDE

ARCHER: a person who uses a bow and arrow

BEGGAR: a person who lives by asking for food or money

BOON: a timely benefit; a blessing

FORESTER: a man hired to guard the forest from outlaws

KNIGHT: a man devoted to the service of a superior, such as a king or lord

LORD: an English nobleman

MAIDEN: an unmarried girl or woman

MARK: an old English unit of currency

MILLER: a person who grinds grain into flour

NOBLEMAN: a man of high rank; an aristocrat

PALFREY (*pahl*-free): a lady's light horse

POTTER: a person who makes pottery

QUARTERSTAFF: a long staff used for fighting

SCORE: twenty things

SCOUNDREL: a rascal, troublemaker

TRADESMAN: a worker in a skilled trade

YEOMAN (*yoh*-mun): a middle-class English landowner

pencil sketch from page 18

FURTHER READING, WEBSITES, AND MOVIES

The Adventures of Robin Hood. DVD. Directed by Michael Curtiz. Hollywood: Warner Bros. Pictures, 1938. This fun and exciting film, starring Errol Flynn as Robin and Olivia De Havilland as Maid Marian, is one of the most popular movies of all time.

Edens, Cooper. *Robin Hood: A Classic Illustrated Edition*. San Francisco: Chronicle Books, 2002. This book features tales of Robin Hood with illustrations dating from the twelfth to the twentieth centuries.

The Geste of Robin Hood
http://web.ics.purdue.edu/~ohlgren/gesttrans.html
Visit this website to read a contemporary translation of one of the original ballads of Robin Hood's adventures. The original geste (folk song) was composed in Middle English in the fifteenth century.

Pyle, Howard. *The Merry Adventures of Robin Hood*. New York: Signet Classics, 1986. Howard Pyle's illustrated adaptations of the Robin Hood stories are some of the most famous and popular in the world.

Robin Hood. DVD. Directed by John Irvin. Hollywood: 20th Century Fox, 1991. This action-packed made-for-TV movie stars Patrick Bergin as Robin and Uma Thurman as Maid Marian.

Robin Hood: A Beginner's Guide to Robin Hood
http://www.boldoutlaw.com/robbeg/robbeg1.html
This Web page provides a brief overview of the legend of Robin Hood and his many adventures. The page is part of a larger site that features a great deal of helpful information about the Outlaw of Sherwood.

CREATING *ROBIN HOOD: OUTLAW OF SHERWOOD FOREST*

Author Paul D. Storrie relied heavily on the earliest versions of the Robin Hood stories available: the lyrics to the medieval songs about Robin and his followers. His research also included the excellent books *Robin Hood* by J. C. Holt and *Robin Hood: A Complete Study of the English Outlaw* by Stephen Thomas Knight. Artist Thomas Yeates referred to modern sources of medieval dress as well as to illustrations by great artists of the past, including Howard Pyle, Harold Foster, and N. C. Wyeth. Professor Andrew Scheil of the University of Minnesota lent his time and expertise in reviewing this project.

INDEX

ABOUT THE AUTHOR AND THE ARTIST

PAUL D. STORRIE was born and raised in Detroit, Michigan, and has returned to live there again and again after living in other cities and states. He has been a fan of Robin Hood tales his entire life, and his very first published work was the 1987 comic book series Robyn of Sherwood about the daughter of the legendary archer. Since then, he has written several comic book stories about Robin Hood himself. His other works includes *Batman Beyond*, *Justice League Adventures*, and *Gotham Girls* for DC Comics and contributions to *Captain America: Red, White & Blue* and *Mutant X: Dangerous Decisions* for Marvel. He has also written *Hercules: The Twelve Labors* in the Graphic Myths and Legends series.

THOMAS YEATES Originally from Sacramento, California, Thomas Yeates began his art training in high school and continued it at Utah State University and at Sacramento State. Subsequently, he was a member of the first class at Joe Kubert's School, a trade program for aspiring comic book artists in New Jersey. Yeates is strongly influenced in his craft by old-guard illustrators like Hal Foster, N. C. Wyeth, and Wallace Wood. He has worked as an illustrator for DC, Marvel, Dark Horse, and many other companies, drawing *Tarzan*, *Zorro*, *the Swamp Thing*, *Timespirits*, *Captain America*, and *Conan*, among others. He has also edited *Al Williamson: Hidden Lands* for Dark Horse.